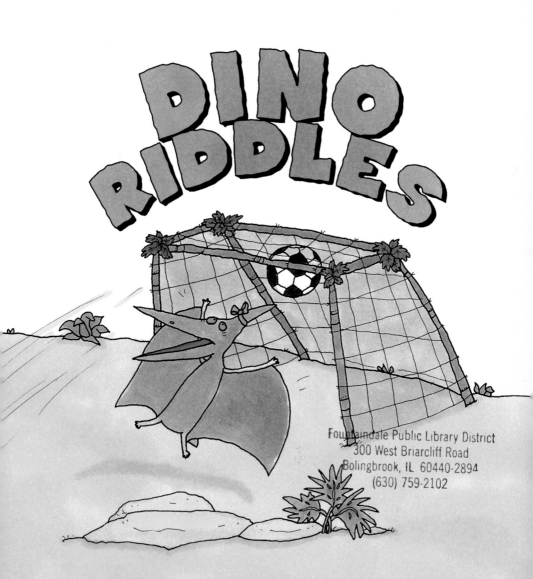

DINO RIDDLES

by Katy Hall and Lisa Eisenberg

pictures by Nicole Rubel

Dial easy-to-read

Dial Books for Young Readers • New York

Published by Dial Books for Young Readers
A division of Penguin Putnam Inc.
345 Hudson Street
New York, New York 10014

The Dial Easy-to-Read logo is a registered trademark of
Dial Books for Young Readers,
a division of Penguin Putnam Inc.
® TM 1,162,718.
1 3 5 7 9 10 8 6 4 2

Library of Congress Cataloging-in-Publication Data
Hall, Katy.
Dino riddles/by Katy Hall and Lisa Eisenberg;
pictures by Nicole Rubel.—1st ed.
p. cm.
Summary: A collection of riddles relating to dinosaurs, such as
"What do you get if you cross a dinosaur with a rabbit? Tricera*hops*!"
and "What do dinosaur campers cook over the fire? Dino-*s'mores*!"
ISBN 0-8037-2239-7
1. Riddles, Juvenile. 2. Dinosaurs—Juvenile humor.
[1. Dinosaurs—Wit and humor. 2. Riddles. 3. Jokes.]
I. Eisenberg, Lisa. II. Rubel, Nicole, ill. III. Title.
PN6371.5.H3477   2002
818'.5402—dc21   97-49947   CIP   AC

Reading Level 2.6

The paintings, which consist of black ink and colored markers,
are color-separated and reproduced in full color.

To Joshua Mactey-don and
Zachary Tricera-schwabs

L.E.

To Ripton Gruss Rosen and
Morgan Gruss Rosen

K.H.

To all the little dinos

N.R.

What do you call a dinosaur in a cowboy hat and spurs?

Tyrannosaurus Tex.

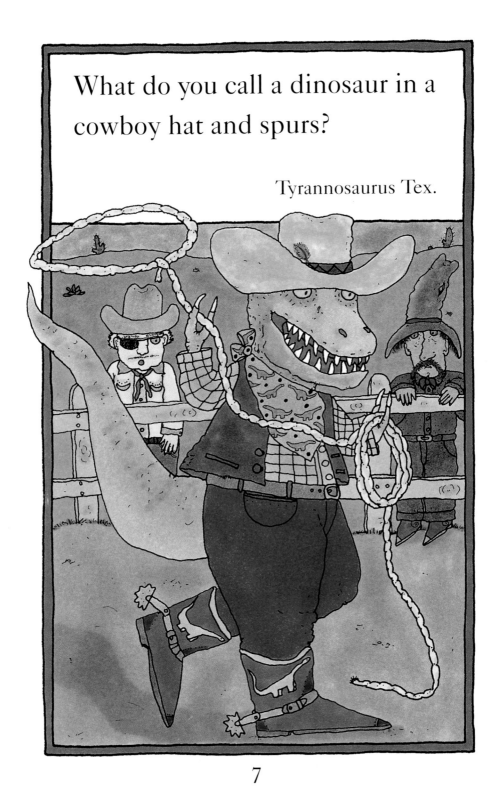

How can you tell if a dinosaur
is a meat-eater or a plant-eater?

Lie down on a plate and see what happens!

What do you call a sleeping dinosaur?

A Stego-*snore*-us.

Who always has change for a
dollar?

A *Dime*-o-saur.

What do you get if you cross a
T. Rex with another T. Rex?

Don't do it! T. Rexes hate to be
double-crossed!

When did the Raptor cross
the street?

When the sign said "Stalk."

How did a stone-age wrecking
crew blast through mountains?

With *dino*-mite!

Which dinosaur plays a mean boogie-woogie?

*Piano*saurus Rex.

What do dinosaurs put on their valentines before they mail them?

Stomps.

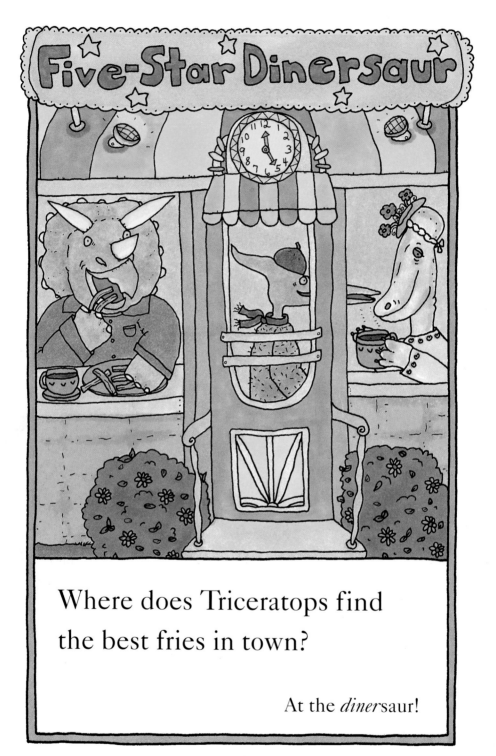

Where does Triceratops find
the best fries in town?

At the *diner*saur!

Why was Stegosaurus the star
of her volleyball team?

She could really *spike* the ball!

Which dinosaur never quits?

*Try*ceratops.

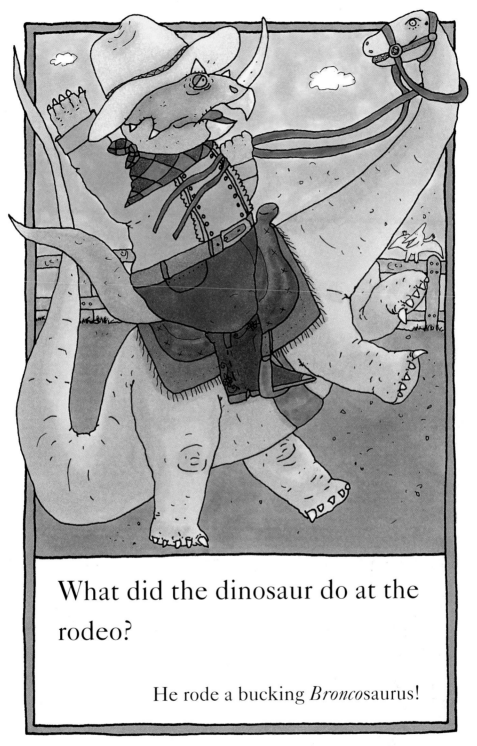

What did the dinosaur do at the rodeo?

He rode a bucking *Bronco*saurus!

What did the little dinosaur get
for her birthday?

A *Toy*rannosaurus Rex.

Which giant reptile has magic powers?

The Dino*sorcerer*.

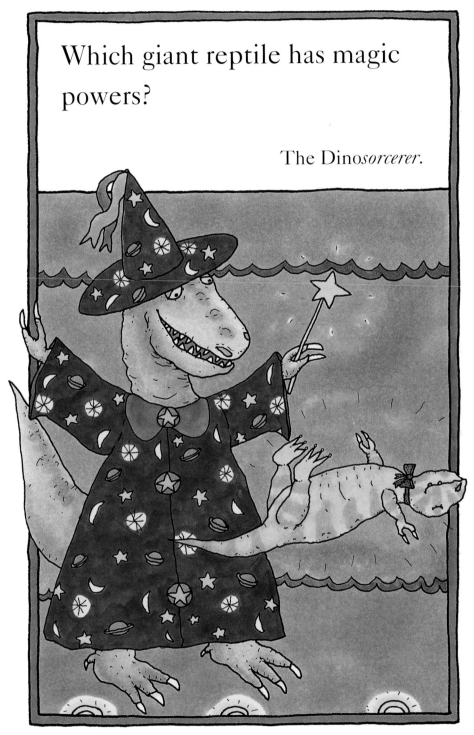

What's the best way to raise a
baby dinosaur?

With a crane.

Do any of the dinosaurs have trunks?

Only the ones who go on vacation!

What did the other dinosaurs
think of Stegosaurus's new
clothes?

They thought he looked really *sharp*.

What should you do if you see a blue dinosaur?

Cheer him up!

What do you get if you cross a
fierce dinosaur and a giraffe?

A Tyrannosaurus Necks.

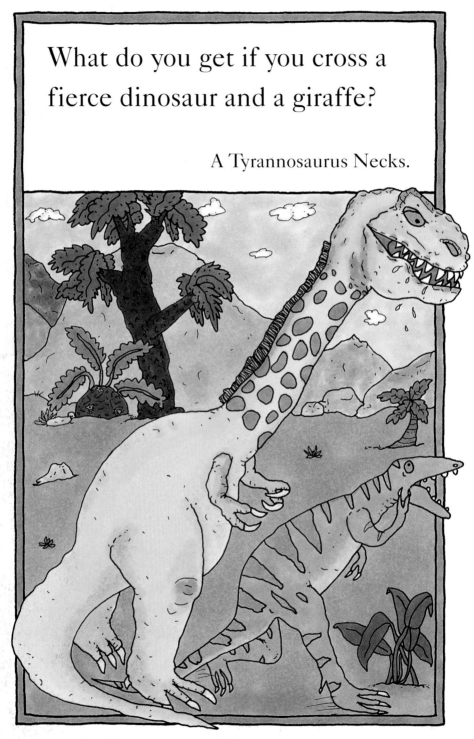

What did the Raptors say when the volcano erupted?

"What a *lava*ly day!"

What did the little dinosaur say when she had three tests to study for?

"I'm swamped!"

What do you get if you cross a dog with a flying reptile?

A *Terrier*dactyl.

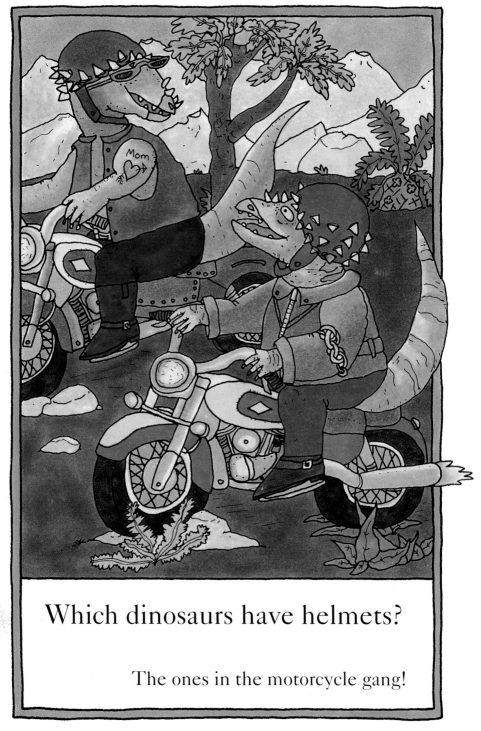

Which dinosaurs have helmets?

The ones in the motorcycle gang!

What did the little dinosaurs
say to the big dinosaur when
she went into the swamp?

"Wade for us!"

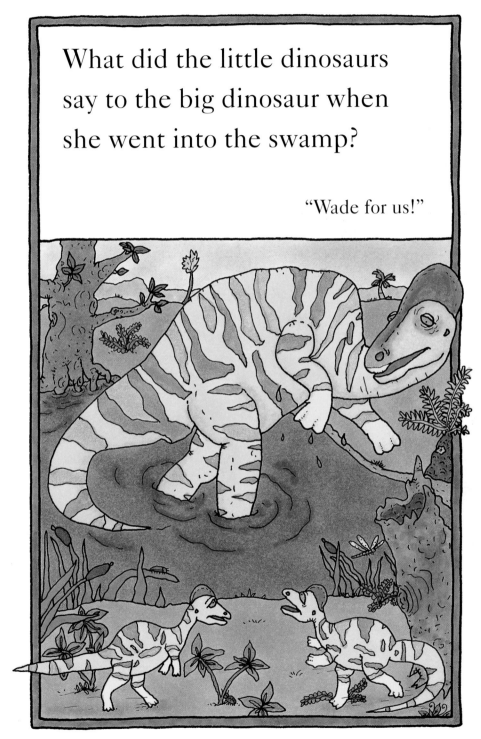

What did the dinosaur put on his barbecued ribs?

Dino*sauce*.

What do you get if you cross a dinosaur with a rabbit?

Tricera*hops*!

What do dinosaurs have that no other animal has?

Baby dinosaurs.

What did the Tyrannosaurus Rex do when she saw the perfect bathing suit?

She snapped it up!

Which dinosaur was a big hit at
the Jurassic Halloween party?

The *Terror*dactyl.

What do dinosaur campers
cook over the fire?

Dino-*s'mores*!

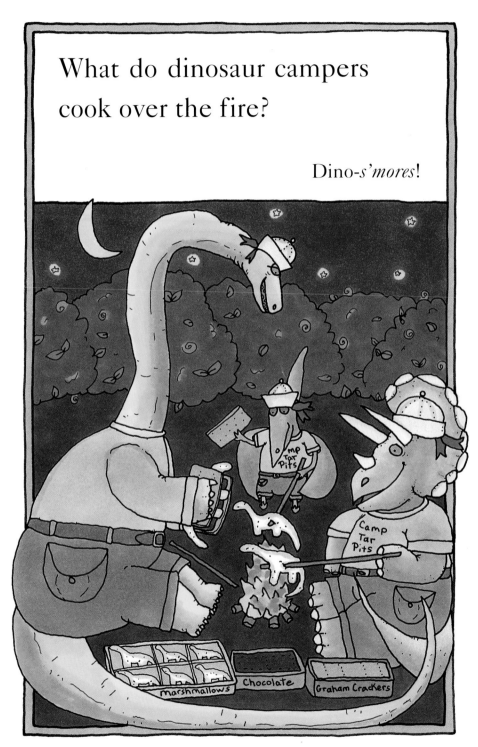

Should you ever write a book
on dinosaurs?

No! You should write a book on paper!

What do you call a T. Rex who tries to find out secrets?

*Spy*rannosaurus Rex.

What kind of bedtime story do dinosaurs like best?

Tall *tails*!